An Autobiography of a Cambria House

How I Became the Cambria Historical Museum

as told to

Ken Renshaw

An Autobiography of a Cambria House

All photos credited to Cambria Historical Society unless otherwise indicated.

Copyright © 2014, 2018 Ken Renshaw
Second Edition 2018
Cover design by Heather UpChurch

Copyright Assigned to
Cambria Historical Society
PO Box 906
Cambria, CA 93428

ISBN-978-0-9852731-8-7

Published by
Constellation Press
1790 Ogden Dr.
Cambria, CA 93428

Table of Contents

Note From Ken Renshaw

I listened.

She told me her story:

1

Humble Beginnings

I am an old house now known as the Cambria Historical Museum in the East Village of Cambria, California. I'm a happy house with many visitors, docents, and caretakers.

I am over a hundred and forty years old and have many stories to tell. My story is part of the story of Cambria.

I will tell you the stories of the people who have lived in me. Since I am very old, I may not remember all the facts of the everyone who lived here. I'll rely on my imagination to fill in what I don't remember to make my story as complete.

Long before they built me, the land I sit on belonged to Spain. Small bands of natives passed by on their way to a tribal village upstream on Santa Rosa Creek The Spanish built their missions inland on the other side of the coastal range, so nobody much came out here. After Mexico declared its independence from Spain in 1821, land grants were made to friends of the Mexican government. In 1841, Juliano Estrada received a grant of around 20 square miles of land, called

Rancho Santa Rosa. The grant included the land that is now Cambria. After California became a state in 1850, the land I stand upon was bought and sold many times. Those are interesting stories, but not my story.

The name of my town changed several times. In the town's early days, It was derisively called Slab Town because the buildings were built with slabs of rough-sawn pine with the tree bark still attached. Locals didn't refer to their town that way. People in San Luis Obispo called it "Slab Town" to put down the upstart town that threatened to become larger and more important than San Luis Obispo.

When the town applied to have a post office, it had to adopt an official name. Locals tried the names of Rosaville, Santa Rosa, and San Simeon, but they were taken. A man who had lived in a similar-looking place in Cambria County, Pennsylvania suggested Cambria. The name wasn't taken by another post office in California, so the U.S. Post Office accepted the name.. In 1870, the town became Cambria, an official place with a post office.

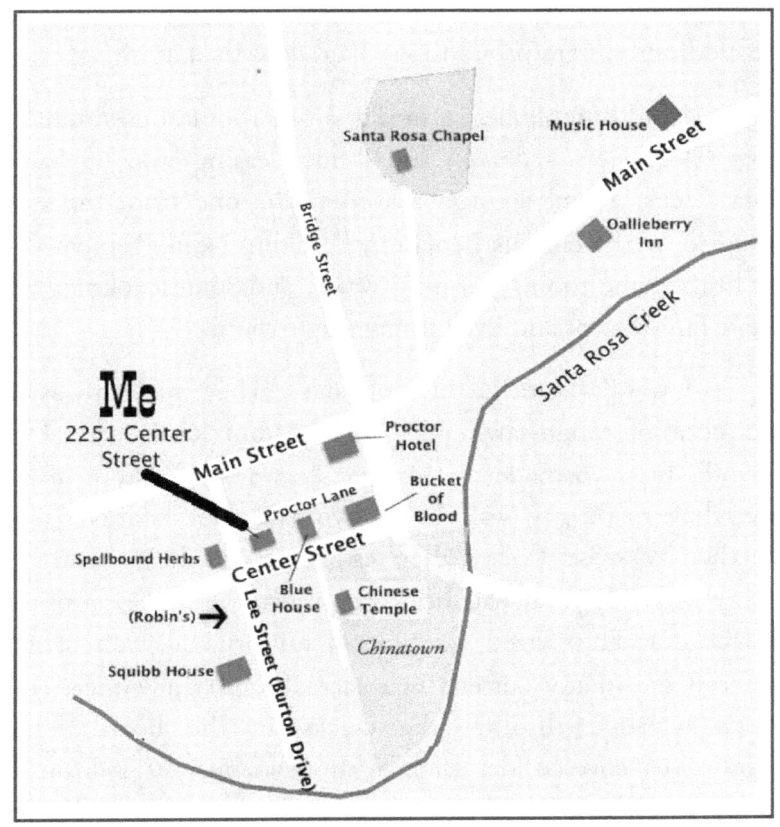

Map of Cambria 1870

They built me in 1870. I am not the oldest house still standing in Cambria. Several houses along Main Street came before me. George Lull built a store with a residence on the second floor five years before 1870. I have heard it's now called the Music House. It is across the street and east of the Olallieberry Inn, built in 1875. Houses that are now parts of the Bluebird Inn and The Brambles were built around the same time as me. The Squibb house, as it is now called, came seven years after me. I don't remember about all the original houses in town. My gift shop has a book that is a self-guided tour of the old houses. I am proud to say I am described in it!

I had humble beginnings as a one-room house built for Tom Clendenen, a drayer, and farmer leasing land up Santa Rosa Creek. I had an iron stove, maybe one from the East designed by the famous Benjamin Franklin–I can't remember–for heating the room, warming water, and some cooking. His whole family slept and lived in my single room.

I wasn't beautiful in those days. They made my walls and floor of rough-sawn pine boards from local trees. Two sawmills in town made my lumber. As was the custom of the day, they made my walls with two layers of boards nailed together crosswise. (When they restored me in 2003, nearly all of my original wood had been eaten away by mice, termites, and beetles. They saved a section of my original walls, which you can see in my current Fireplace Room.) In winter, cold winds whistled through the cracks in the boards. The Clendenens covered the walls with newspaper as a form of decorative wallpaper and to keep the cold out.

My water was hand-pumped from a well in the backyard. In those days, indoor plumbing didn't exist. The bathroom was a privy in the bac yard.

Thank goodness Mrs. Clendenen cooked on a wood stove in another shack in the back yard. That shack caught fire and burned. If the kitchen had been in me, I would have burned down.

I was a noisy house with four little children and their parents all living in my single room. Mrs. Clendenen acted sadly. Diphtheria took one of her children while they lived in me. In Mrs. Clendenen's lifetime, including times when she lived elsewhere, she had ten children, six of whom died young. Think of all the birthdays she could remember but didn't celebrate.

During my early days, I saw many amazing sights. The Civil War had ended only a few years before, and discharged soldiers had come out west. Stern-faced men in dirty blue or gray uniform jackets passed by carrying their rifles. Miners from the mines in the nearby mountains passed by on the way to spending their pay at one of the five saloons on Main Street.

Real estate entrepreneurs dressed in fancy suits and hats make deals for land and buildings. Workers passed by me hauling boards to building sites. Buildings rose up near me, including a blacksmith shop on Bridge Street, a wheelwright shop that could repair wagons or buggies (where the current post office parking lot is), and dry goods stores on Main Street. If you looked east of me on Proctor Lane, the alley that runs beside me, you'd see the three-story Proctor Hotel, the largest hotel in the county.

Wagons loaded with logs passed by me on their way to the sawmills. Carts of timber used to support mine shafts and firewood for the quicksilver kilns rattled by on their way to the mountains.

Stage leaving Wells Fargo office

The stagecoach that brought mail on its route from San Luis Obispo to San Simeon stopped at the Wells Fargo office in the Franklin building in back of me on Main Street directly Bridge Street didn't end at the community cemetery as it does now. It was part of the original Old Coast Road that led to San Simeon.

For a while, Cambria flourished as one of the major ports of San Luis Obispo County. Loads of farm products passed by me on their way to be shipped to San Francisco and other California ports. At Leffingwell Landing, near the north end of today's Moonstone Beach Drive, men carried products through the surf and loaded them onto longboats, Seamen rowed to ships anchored off-shore. After 1869, when George Hearst built a long pier in San Simeon, cargo could be unloaded from longboats or small ships directly to wagons. Even though shippers had to pay a fee for using the pier, most of the shipping went there.

Cambria became a boomtown because of the port activity and mining. The boom brought real estate speculation. In 1871, Mr. Clenden sold me to the hotelier and real estate speculators Winfield S. Whittaker and Jobe E. Apsey.

However, I was lonely. After Mr. Clenden sold me I was empty. I had no neighbors. I heard carpenters building other houses and stores around town. Imagine my delight when a real estate speculator built a house near me on Center street. It had one room in front and two in back. The town Doctor, Dr. Parkhurst and his wife, Mary bought it. She was gorgeous and elegant. I admired her as she took her daily walk by me. Children and others watched her and tried to imitate her poise and perfect posture.

My new owners, Whittaker and Apsey thought a few improvements would make me more valuable. They added a bedroom on the Proctor Lane (north) side of the house, again using single wall construction. They replaced my pine flooring with imported, more durable, fir boards. They added a porch on the Center Street side of me to give me style.

I was grateful to Whittaker and Apsey because they spruced me up from being a shack to looking like a proper house. I now looked similar to the style of house in New England referred to as "salt box."

They sold me in 1873 to a man from Massachusetts named Leonidas Root. I remember little of him except that he called his Irish wife Anna, and worked hard as a farmer. In 1882, he sold me to Benjamin H. Franklin and moved to Arizona.

2

I Come of Age

The Benjamin H. Franklin who bought me was not a descendant of the Founding Father of the same name. That didn't stop him from giving people the impression he was. His great-grandfather, also named Benjamin, lived in New Jersey. I guess many Franklin families had children named Benjamin.

The Benjamin Franklin who owned me came to San Francisco at age six years. He later studied in San Jose to become a school teacher. He taught school in San Simeon before he became an attorney and started investing in business ventures. Although he never lived in me, he did me proud. He added my parlor, two bedrooms (now used as a gift shop and exhibit room), and front and back porches. He added the fireplace, windows and interior trim, and rearranged interior walls. It only took ten months! When it was over, I felt beautiful.

Benjamin Franklin doubled his money when he sold me to Sarah Woods Guthrie. Sarah Woods Guthrie fell in love with me when she first saw me after Mr. Franklin's remodeled. She bought me in 1883 while her husband, Samuel, was on a business trip to San Francisco. Only her name appeared on the

Sarah Woods Guthrie

deed. I don't know where she got the money. Perhaps she bought me to assert her independence.

She loved me and made an unending string of minor improvements. I loved it when she planted my garden with roses, lilies, and narcissi. Sarah delighted in roses. She was excited when she found a different variety to plant. She loved the Duchesse de Brabant roses that still grow by my front door today. Almost all the roses that grow in my garden today are descendants of those planted by Sarah. They, like me, have survived over a hundred years with little care.

The Guthries were prosperous people. Samuel became a manager and then a partner of the Grant and Lull Store at the corner of Bridge and Main Street. He also worked as an accountant at the Oceanic Mine. Having had his hand on the pulse of the real estate and boom and the mining boom. He invested wisely.

Samuel Guthrie

These were happy times for me. They replaced doors and windows. They added trim detail to my outside. I gleamed in new coats of paint. They decorated my interior with beautiful furnishings. I loved being fussed over!

Dr. Parkhurst and his wife, Mary were my neighbors until 1894. They seemed happy and were friends of the Guthries. Sarah talked to Mary often, and they shared many ideas on how to decorate me. I don't know why they sold the house and moved away.

My new neighbors, Louis and Lala Maggetti, couldn't become close friends with the Guthries. Lala had to tend to her six noisy children. Louis spent a lot of time in his leather goods shop on Main Street Sometimes the girls would sneak into my garden and pick flowers. Louis added a second story for the children as they got older. He was a frugal man–he had to be to feed all those kids–so he only made the staircase 23 inches wide. Louis and later his adult kids lived in the house for forty years.

A photo of me taken about 1890. Pictured are Mr. Guthrie, his wife Sarah (at the top of the stairs), and two of Sarah's sisters, Margaret Woos Ott and May Woods Leffingwell.

Samuel Guthrie died in 1905. Sarah and I became sad. I didn't receive much in the way of improvements or care over the next few years.

The street in front of me, running from the creek to Main Street, is Lee Street. The earliest Cambria maps show that to be true. Lee street stopped at the creek until 1888 when they built the first bridge. Before that, people wanting to cross Santa Rosa Creek had to ford the creek at the bottom of Bridge Street or use one the toll walking bridges at each end of Main Street. There never was a bridge across the creek at Bridge Street. Drainage ditches on each side of Bridge Street carried water runoff from the springs and ranch uphill. Each house had a small bridge across the ditch to allow people to walk from the front yard to the center of the street. The street should have been named The Street of Many Bridges.

The County rerouted the Coast Highway to bypass Cambria in 1961. Streets were renamed. Lee Street became Burton Drive in the 1970s. By that time, I was a hundred years old. I don't accept the new name-it will always be Lee Street to me.

3

Swiss-American Parades

The magnificent Swiss-American summer parades in the 1870s started on Lee Street. The parade formed up near the creek on Lee Street, near the place now called The Brambles. The Cambria Brass Band led the parade, followed by men on horseback and decorated horse-drawn floats. One float carried young girls in elaborate costumes portraying the virtues of *Liberty, Prosperity*, and *Truth*.

Liberty, Prosperity, and Truth

The parade came up Lee Street, and then turned right in front of me on to.Center Street. At Bridge Street it turned north to pass the post office. The band was loud and magnificent and made my windows rattle.

Cambria Brass Band

They named the Swiss-American Parade to honor the early Swiss dairy farmers who were a mainstay of Cambria's economy from the 1870s until the 1930s. They produced butter and loaded it onto ships bound for the lucrative market in San Francisco. By contrast, mining was a boom and bust business depending on the price of mercury or the quality of ore being mined.

Procession to Phelan Grove

Hundreds of wagons of visitors and locals joined in behind the Swiss-American Parade at Main Street and headed out to a gala community picnic north of town.

Thousands of people came to Cambria for its celebration just as they now do for Pinedorado. When the celebration grew, it moved farther out Bridge Street, to near where the cemetery is now.. At *Phelan Grove.* they held a giant barbecue, listened to long-winded speeches by politicians, played baseball, watched a rodeo, and danced. For many families, spread throughout the county, it was a family reunion.

Gathering at Phelan Grove 1906

4

The Great Fire

The raucous times of Cambria came to a sudden end early in the morning of October 1, 1889. The year had been hot and dry. My well went dry, and the Guthries had someone come and dig it deeper. Guests of the Guthries talked of the large forest fire they had seen from a ship while sailing from Monterey to Cambria. At night, I could hear the boards of the buildings along Main Street creak in the dry wind. Sand blew in from the beach and coated the streets. Dust from Lee Street blew into my parlor.

Early in the morning the dreaded cries of "Fire!" rang out. I saw flames as high as a building down Proctor Lane from me. The hotel's wood pile, stacked high for the winter, was on fire. Soon the hotel was engulfed. Cries of "Help!" came from a guest trapped on the second story of the hotel. Men found and placed a ladder against the side of the hotel and saved the guest moments before the whole hotel exploded in flames. It terrified me when the Proctor Hotel roof collapsed with a boom sending a tower of embers into the air. The falling embers ignited buildings on the other side of Bridge and Main Streets. Cambria had one water tank, but nobody could make the hose connected to it work. The flames spread unabated from one dry pine wood building to the next. Within minutes the entire business district was aflame. Townspeople helped businessmen carry inventory out of the buildings that were not engulfed in flames.

Mrs. Guthrie and I watched in horror as the buildings across Proctor Lane behind me burned to the ground. The heat singed my siding, but I didn't catch on fire. People came to try to pump water from my dry well. My privy burned. My cook shack ignited, and then somebody put the fire out by shoveling dirt on it.

Main and Bridge Streets were a bonfire. Almost every business went up in flames. Two general stores burned, along with three saloons, two hotels, a blacksmith shop, a livery stable, a paint store, a lumberyard and furniture store, a hardware store, the offices of the doctor, the office of the newspaper, and the Cambrian Hall (the largest meeting place in the county). Six of the fifty downtown homes burned. No one was injured or died in the fire. The only casualty was a horse that had been led from Campbell's burning livery stable. The horse pulled free from the boy who was holding it and ran back into the burning stable. The Onlookers shouted and screamed in horror. The horse died without making a sound.

Main Street After The Great Fire

The Great Fire was over in a few hours. As the sun rose, the business district was a smoldering ruin. Carts took away the rescued merchandise from the street.

Benjamin Franklin came and sat on my porch and drank lemonade that Mrs. Guthrie offered. He had lost four uninsured buildings on Main Street but was not without hope. As a businessman, he saw opportunity in the ashes and talked of rebuilding bigger and better.

Men had saved the contents of the post office. Before the fire had stopped smoking, men made a make shift Cambria post office in the street across from where the Proctor Hotel had been. We were still a town!

Main Street in the 1890s after being rebuilt

New buildings soon replaced the burnt out shells of buildings and ashes. Within a year the signs of The Great Fire disappeared.

The new buildings reflected a change in the economy. The decline of mining lowered the need for saloons and entertainment for miners. Farm implements and dairy equipment replaced miners' picks in the new stores.

Mrs. Guthrie had to replant my garden. She saved most of my roses. Since her family was from Oregon, she planted the Elephant Garlic and the Port Orford Cedar from Oregon in my backyard. They still live. In the wild, Port Orford Cedar can live several hundred years. This one is still a baby.

5

My Chinese Neighbors

I loved my Chinese neighbors across Center Street from me. The people were so interesting. When the Guthries lived in me, there many Chinese men lived in the county around Cambria. Some worked in the mines, and others worked on solitary kelp farms and lived in shacks spread along the coast from Cayucos to the north of San Simeon. Back then, California had a law that forbid Chinese men from having wives. Chinese bachelors came to Cambria on weekends to shop at the two grocery stores and to socialize. The land on the other side of Center Street from me,-now Greenspace's Creekside Reserve- was their community center.

A woman who moved to San Francisco after her husband's death owned the land. She did not care if the Chinese squatted on her land. The Chinese built a few dilapidated shacks that people lived in, a laundry, and a social hall that served as a Temple. Mr. Guthrie said he visited a shack there and saw men lying on bunk beds smoking opium. I could often hear loud shouting late at night as they gambled. Mr.

Guthrie said they played Fan-tan and other games of chance. They gambled a lot.

One highlight of my year was the celebration of Chinese New Year. I relished the aromas from deep pit barbecues and pots of foods that wafted my way. One time, one of the Guthrie's friends brought them a basket of roasted pig. After their benefactor left, the Gutheries tried to eat the gift, but the Chinese spices were too strong for their American taste.

During the New Year celebration, raucous gambling continued all night. A fireworks display climaxed the celebration. Cambrians from all over town lined Center Street to peer into the Chinese celebration and see the show. I was terrified by the fireworks that reminded me of The Great Fire. The next day, the area was deserted. Everyone had gone back to their isolated existence.

By the time Sarah Guthrie sold the house to the Bianchinis in 1916, the Chinese community center disappeared. William Warren bought the land that had bee used by the Chinese. He drove the Chinese squatters from the property and pushed their laundry building and shacks into the creek.

The Warren property included a house near Center Street. Then, houses like me were only loosely connected to their foundations. They were carted or dragged from one place to another. The Warrens bought a building that had been Cambria's first high school at the corner of Lee and Main Street. You can imagine my surprise when I saw it being towed by a team of horses down Lee Street in front of me. When they tried to go from Lee Street to Center Street, the house could not make the turn. The movers tore down my fence at the corner and dragged the schoolhouse over part of my beautiful gardens to make the turn. I was furious. After the house was in place, William Warren and his son joined the school with the existing house on Center Street.

Later, the Warrens decided they needed more room. They moved the Temple from where it had been, closer to the creek, and grafted it onto the back of the other two structures. It was fascinating to watch.

Members of the Warren family lived in the house until 1964, using the Temple as another room in the house. Later, the Warrens moved to another house next door. I despaired as the house with the Temple fell into disrepair and started to disintegrate. I feared that would be my fate.

Temple (bulge at the far right) as part of Warren house in 1980 (Tribune Photo)

Cambria Greenspace, a local land conservation trust, knew of the historic value of the Temple. They bought the property, extracted the Temple structure, moved it to the park across from me, and restored it.

*Chinese Temple in
Cambria's
Creekside Reserve
(Greenspace photo)*

*Buddhist priest rededicating Temple
(Hind Foundation photo)*

In 2008, the memory of my Chinese neighbors returned. As I watched, a Buddhist priest rang gongs, burned incense, and lead dancing dragons and attendees around the building to rededicate the Temple. The ceremony brought back my memories of the good times.

6

The Bianchinis Buy Me

After Samuel Guthrie died in 1905, Sarah and I became very sad. Before then, I had been the venue of many dinner parties with other businessmen and visitors. Suddenly, Sarah and I felt empty. Sarah often left me to visit relatives and went live near of them. In 1914, after being unoccupied most of the time, I was leased to Eugenio and Louisa Bizzini Bianchini.

Two years later, Sarah remarried. She sold me to the Bianchinis. The bill of sale said $10. I was not insulted because they paid more for me. In those days, people figured the amount of money exchanged in large transactions was of nobody else's business–definitely not the business of people in the County Recorder's Office who levied a property transfer tax based on the sale price.

It took a while to get used to the Bianchinis after they moved in. I had relished the peace and quiet while Sarah was away. Eugenio had many colorful friends from his multifaceted

Eugenio and Louisa Bizzini Bianchini

careers as butcher, dairyman, bootlegger, mine owner, and real estate speculator. You should have seen the drinking parties in my parlor! He avoided paying the federal tax on liquor with his bootlegging. He imported bootleg whiskey at a sandy beach north of the Piedras Blancas lighthouse. He stored it in a cellar he had dug under me. He continued his bootlegging throughout the 1919 to 1931 Prohibition.

His friend, "Doc" Billy Randall, had a drug store on Main Street. "Doc" Randall sold "tonics" to anyone who came in and complained of a malady.

Being an immigrant from Switzerland, Eugenio was a wholehearted participant in the Swiss-American summer festivities.

Eugenio Bianchini, Master of the Barbecue, at Phelan Grove

Because of his career as a butcher, he became Master of the Barbecue. The Hearst family donated several head of cattle that he butchered, cut into fifty-pound hunks, and roasted for hours over an open pit barbecue. Eugenio used a secret barbecue sauce, which included Elephant Garlic Sarah Gutherie had planted in my garden (and is still growing out there today) for the sauce. The recipe is thought to have included many of the "flavorings" from my cellar. His fame as a barbecue chef grew and he was called upon to be in charge of many other important barbecues in the county.

The Klau Mine
(Located in Adelaida between Cambria and Paso Robles)

When World War I broke out, the price of mercury soared because it was used in munitions. Eugenio became a partner and then the manager of the Klau Mine. It made a lot of money for Eugenio during the war.

He bought a 100-acre dairy with a house at the mouth of Pico Creek for his daughter, Elvira, and her husband, Rocco Rava. (After World War II, in the final settlement of Eugenio's estate, the property was sold to a real estate developer. It became San Simeon Acres.)

Louisa and Eugenio had seven children over fourteen years from 1889 to 1904. Thank goodness that by the time Louisa and Eugenio moved into me they only had one nine-year-old child living at home. Later, he was nicknamed Weasel. I don't know how or why he got that nickname. Every boy seemed to acquire nicknames back then.

My property originally ended at the Cedar tree, at the edge of the bricks now by my east porch. There was another shack in the lot beyond the Cedar tree. Eugenio bought the shack and tore it down.

Louisa and Eugenio left me and moved to Cayucos. Three of the boys, William (Spider), James (Weasel), and Walter (Coyote), lived in me for a long time. They drank a lot of whiskey. After watching them all those years, I have come to believe the three boys were ruined by the easily available whiskey in the house. One of their drinking buddies was Art Beal, the builder of Cambria's Nitt Witt Ridge.

They "cured" their hangovers from drinking too much whiskey by drinking Milk of Magnesia, which came in blue bottles.

When the Cambria Historical Society was doing an archeological survey of me, they found a huge pile of the blue bottles in a pit in my backyard.

The one good thing I can say about them is they never missed a day of work as mine and ranch laborers, no matter how bad of shape they were in.

After my long time next-door neighbor, Louis died in 1935, the little blue house was sold to Elvira Bianchini Rava and her husband, an Italian emigrant Rocco Rava who worked for Eugenio Bianchini. Elvira was grown and not living with her parents when they owned me.

Roco had a hobby business of selling mushrooms to restaurants in San Francisco. He would pick them in the pine forest, bring them home and dry them on the fence around his house. I loved the smell of the drying mushrooms on the warm days when the wind blew my direction from the little blue house.

7

World War II

I know little about this World War II. I heard people talking about it and how it changed their lives. Spider listened to the radio while he sat in a rocking chair after coming home from drinking whiskey at Camozzi's Saloon. As far as I could tell, some people called Japanese bombed the ships in a place called Pearl Harbor, not far from here in the ocean, on December 7, 1941. I didn't understand how or why these Japanese people did that. Everyone feared Cambria might be next. I figured I'd be bombed because I was next to Main Street.

The War came to Cambria only two weeks later when something they called a submarine sank an oil tanker, the Montebello, a few miles out to sea from Moonstone Beach. It was six o'clock in the morning. Everyone in town heard gunfire and explosions and ran into the streets. I was terrified because I thought the bombing of Cambria had started. Men carrying their shotguns or rifles jumped into cars or trucks and headed for the shore. Women gathered their children up and hid in their houses with the window blinds pulled down. In a few hours, men came back and said a ship had been torpedoed and sank.

The submarine fired its deck machine gun at the lifeboats. Then, it slid beneath the waves and disappeared.

The Union Oil Tanker Montebello

Someone came into town and shouted, "Before the Montebello sank, all the crew made it into the lifeboats!" Three of the four lifeboats drifted south in the fog along the coast. People said tugboats rescued the crew down by Cayucos. The Captain of the Montebello rode in the fourth boat. It leaked because it had been machine-gunned by the submarine.

Rescue of the crew of the Montebello during surf landing of lifeboat south of Cambria (Photo by San Luis Obispo Telegram Tribune)

They came ashore on the rocky coast at Wong's Farm, south what is now known as Cambria's Marine Terrace. Cambria men massed on shore to rescue the crew as the lifeboat broke up on the rocks. Heroic rescues occurred No one was lost. In the above picture, you can see the Captain (circled) in the water. Someone swam out to him with a rope. On the shore, men appear to be pulling them to safety.

I heard a triumphant motorcade taking the survivors to the Cambria Pines Lodge. Everybody continued to celebrate their heroism in the bar. After everyone got patched up and given warm clothes, the Highway Patrol took them to the San Luis Sanitarium where the Captain rejoined his crew.

For now, Cambria survived. No Japanese boats came to invade Cambria

A teenager who stayed at the shore when everyone came back, salvaged an eighteen-foot lifeboat oar from the broken lifeboat. The teenager carried the oar home. He moved it with him to various houses for seventy-five years. A few years ago he donated it to the museum. It is now on display in my exhibit room with the story of the Montebello's sinking.

The war changed how Cambrians lived. There was rationing of food and gasoline. People had books of rationing coupons they gave to store clerks when they bought food or other goods. Many people rode horses to save gas. Spider had an old truck that didn't run parked in my backyard along with rusted farm implements, barrels, and metal junk. During a scrap metal drive, men came and took all that stuff away. Spider said they made an Army tank from the old truck. I don't know if that is true.

During the war, Spider put paper over my windows. He said it prevented Japanese from seeing the light and dropping bombs on me. During those years, it was always dark and gloomy inside me. Coyote, Spider, and Weasel seemed to hide from the war. Because all the young men had gone to fight, the Bianchini boys always had work. People said they were always reliable hard workers.

After work, they drank whiskey and listened to radio broadcasts of news about the war. I never understood who the people and places were that the radio described. I knew the war was someplace else, and many people got killed. I never lost the fear the I might be bombed in some sort of sneak attack.

Cambria Pines Lodge about 1942 while taken over by U.S. Army

Coyote, Spider, and Weasel did nothing to maintain me. My beautiful gardens became overgrown with weeds. My paint peeled and my roof leaked. I became a sorrowful sight.

The Army occupied the Cambria Pines Lodge and many soldiers lived there. Nobody ever found out what they did. The soldiers who came to the USO (a civilian-staffed entertainment and social center) in a Main Street storefront would not talk about what they did at the Lodge. People said the soldiers looked more like school teachers than combat troops. An armed guard sat in the lobby twenty-four hours a day. I overheard many rumors about what the rest of the soldiers did. Some said they decoded secret messages from the Japanese. Others said they kept Army records of those who died in the war. People reported seeing civilian cars driven by armed soldiers come and unload locked and sealed boxes. I saw a few soldiers pass by me on the way to the USO but they never looked threatening or carried guns.

After the Montebello sank, the Coast Guard came to patrol the shore. People said the patrolmen had big dogs with them as they walked the bluffs. They never came by me because they lived on the coast.

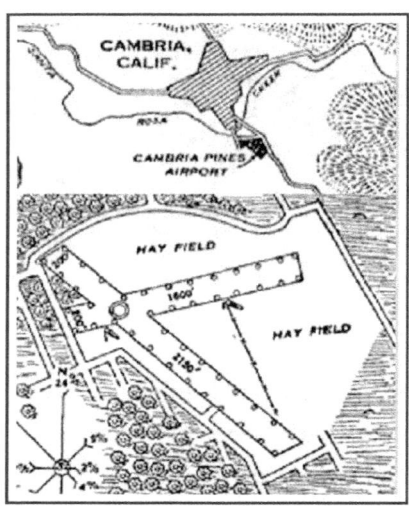

Cambria Airport in the 1930s
(from "Abandoned and Little Known
Airports" website)

Cambria had an airport long before the military took over the Lodge in 1942. In the 1930s, the Cambria Pines Airport was built across the street from the Cambria Pines Lodge so part-time residents could fly in from Los Angeles to their vacation homes. In the drawing, the Cambria Pines Lodge is at the left center, across the road from the airport. The runways were dirt strips mowed in the fields of weeds.

You can imagine my surprise the first time an airplane flew over me in the 1930s. Coyote told Weasel it was a World War I fighter plane like the ones he had seen at an air show. Most of the time, there were only a few airplanes per month. Even after World War II started, there few planes flew over me. Once, a big, brown painted airplane with two noisy engines flew out of there.

Stinson Voyager, Typical Private Airplane of 1946

I recall someone telling Spider that many military pilots took up flying private airplanes after the war. Others, fascinated by the freedom of flight, joined them. For a while after the war, I saw many private airplanes flying over Cambria. At first, I feared some carried bombs. I got used to them. Many people talked of going on airplane rides with friends or relatives. Flying in small planes was a great novelty.

When they built the Highway One bypass of downtown Cambria in the early 1960s, they ran the highway through one of the runways. That ended the Cambria Pines Airport.

I didn't care. I always figured the airplanes were a noisy nuisance.

8

The Legal Tangles

I felt sorry for Eugenio during his last several years. He lived in Cayucos and suffered from diabetes. The last time he visited me he rode in a wheelchair.

His wife had died the year before. He had a leg amputated. The poor man made me sad. He died in 1942, and my years of neglect and decline began.

Eugenio, an experienced businessman, had taken care to have his estate in order before he died. He established a plan for a trust to manage his assets until September 1948, at which time his assets, including me, would be distributed to his seven children. The court appointed Weasel and Spider trustees in 1944. Weasel and Spider didn't care much about legal matters and were content to drink and work and otherwise ignore my maintenance or fate.

Settling Eugenio's trust became very complicated. Elvira, Eugenio's daughter who lived in my little blue house neighbor, died without making a valid will. Her interest in the estate transferred to her husband, Rocco Rava. After Rocco died, in 1975 without a will, his estate had to be divided between relatives in Italy. His financial interest in me inherited from Elvira was included. The little blue house's legal problems became entangled with my own. I never understood how it was settled. During this period of litigation, she was empty and deteriorating. In 1978 local resident Marjorie Meacham Delyear bought the little blue house and saved it from being torn down.She fixed it up, gave it a new coat of blue paint, and rented it out for offices and shops. I was delighted when my current owners , the Cambria Historical Society, bought her, She is my oldest friend.

I never understand all of what Weasel and Spider said about this. I knew many lawyers wrangled over me and Bianchini's other assets.

Me, at my worst

In 1951, Palmira Scott, one of the Bianchini girls, ran across Proctor Lane into the back of Soto's Market and yelled: "Weasel is having trouble breathing!" Later, she returned and said, "His throat is closing up!" Two employees of Soto's loaded Weasel into the back of a market delivery truck and took him across Main Street to the doctor's office.

The doctor tried to do a tracheotomy on him in the back of the truck. Too late! Weasel died.

Two local men, Tom Gerst and Jim Evans, the current owners of the old Bucket of Blood saloon, bought interests in the estate from a collection agent and disgruntled beneficiaries of the trust. By 1969, they had a major interest in my ownership.

I was in bad shape, with my roof collapsing, infested with termites, beetles, and mice, and sliding off my foundation. Nobody took care of me.

Coyote lived in the house until he got lung cancer. He died at the Fresno Veteran's Hospital in 1959. Spider died at home in 1971. After Spider's death, I was abandoned. High school boys broke into me, wrote graffiti on the walls, and left trash everywhere. I became a major eyesore, isolated from the rest of town by a rusty chain-link fence.

Many people played roles in saving me. In 1986, Sharon Lovejoy and Jeff Prostovich bought the building Heart's Ease (now known as Spellbound Herbs), on the other side of Lee Street, or Burton Drive, if you insist. They valued old buildings and began an effort to save me. Sharon used to sneak onto the property at night to water and tend my garden, which had survived without care for forty years. She took a cutting of the Belle of Portugal rose that now grows in front of Spellbound Herbs store. I still enjoy seeing it from across the street. Jeff boarded me up. Vagrants broke in, built fires in makeshift fire pits on my floor, and drew satanic graffiti on my walls. I cheered when the sheriff's deputies kicked them out. I had feared they would set me on fire.

In the 1980s, a group of people thought I should be torn down and made into a parking lot for downtown businesses.

Jeff and a few friends heard a county inspector was coming the next day to see if I was an eyesore and should be torn down. Jeff and friends snuck onto my property during the night and gave me a fresh coat of paint. The inspector determined that someone was maintaining me and I should not be demolished.

The idea of being destroyed terrified me. I had visions of bulldozers showing up, pushing me into a pile of rubble, and dumping me in the creek.

As time dragged on, the beneficiaries wouldn't agree to a settlement of the litigation.

In 1997, Gerst and Evans filed a "Complaint for Partition" an action against the other beneficiaries to force division of the remaining properties. This type of suit calls on all beneficiaries to come forward, state their interests, and then the court determines how to split up the properties.

The litigation with the heirs or owners ended in 1999. The properties of the trust were ordered to be sold. Nobody considered me a bargain.

When potential buyers and building inspectors came around, they said terrible things about me: "a tear-down, a standing trash pile."

My roof leaked for years and my fireplace room floor rotted away. Termites destroyed much of my older structure. One of the corner piers of my rock foundation disappeared, causing me to sag. I could hardly hold myself together. One of the old-time local ranchers volunteered to hook up a team of horses and drag me into the creek. The next winter creek's flood would sweep me out to sea.

I didn't understand that Priscilla Comen, another person who wanted me saved, had placed me on The National Register of Historic Places. My being on that list created a cloud of uncertainty whether the County would allow me to be demolished without an owner going over many expensive, time-consuming, and maybe unsurmountable legal hurdles.

One of the biggest hurdles would be getting permission to destroy my heritage garden. It contained many unique species of roses and other plants. Nobody expected to make a quick buck by buying me. Everyone walked away from me shaking their heads.

Few people understood that I had a secret asset: my water connection. The Cambria Community Services District, which supplies water to the community, declared a water emergency. Additional residential water connections were forbidden.

But, a loophole in the rules existed. If someone wanted to build a new house, they could buy the connection rights of another house and "move" the water connection to the construction site. Before the moratorium, people obtained connection rights for houses never built. Those connection rights could also be "moved." At the time I was on the market, connection rights sold for $125,000!

I didn't understand all of this, but the real estate appraiser who decided my sale price did. I went on the market for half a million dollars! A builder could have bought me for the asking price and "moved" my water connection. However, they would be stuck with the National Register of Historic Places legal hassles and cost of getting rid of me.

The valuation flattered me. I still feared I would stay untended until I was in such bad repair that the County would allow me to be demolished in spite of my listing on the National Register of Historic Places.

People laughed at me when I came on the market in 1999. "That dilapidated and falling down house is priced at a half million dollars."

Priscilla Comen's document that nominated me to the U.S. Department of Interior's National Park Service as a Historic Place made these points: I was significant because I'm a visual reminder of the early pattern of development of a rural town. I'm on the block directly south of Main Street. In rural towns, the businesses stood on the Main Street. The residential areas developed on streets parallel to the main street, creating a natural zoning. Residential lots were larger than those on the main street and houses had setbacks from their boundaries.

She claimed the most unusual aspect of me is how I document the growth of nineteenth-century building technology. I started out as a simple square shack and was added onto, modernized, and embellished with time.

I always thought of myself as just another house.

9

My Salvation

Since no one bid on me, while I was listed with a real estate agent, I was to be sold at auction on the County Court House steps. When I heard, I was filled with fear. Who would buy me?

Long before the auction, the Cambria Historical Society raised money to buy me. They called me a cultural resource. I was surprised one day when I heard members of the Cambria Historical Society standing in front of me, dressed in long dresses and hats like the Bianchinis wore in 1916, telling passers-by of my history. Other people dressed as they did in the good old days stood in front of the blue house next to me telling its story. Someone said people were standing in front of houses my age all over town dressed in period clothes telling the stories of those houses. The Historical Society was conducting a creative fundraiser for donations to help buy me. That news cheered me up. Maybe I had a future!

The Historical Society didn't have the $500,000 in spare change in its cash box. Small donations did not accumulate fast enough. Time for heroic efforts!

I heard Kathe Tanner, then president of the Historical Society and her husband, Richard were searching for grants. The California Department of Transportation (Caltrans) had a pot of money reserved for Transportation Enhancement Activities. They'd make grants for projects that made destinations like Cambria more interesting. Kathe applied for a grant, offering to have a display room in the museum that documented the construction of Highway One from Carmel to San Simeon. At the last minute before the deadline for the grant application, Kathe found out grants were not usually made to a museum unless it was a transportation-related museum. I was a house!

Information kiosk

Kathe changed the application and proposal at the last minute. She added the kiosk in my yard that shows trails and other walking and biking opportunities. Then, she made the proposal

Visitors waiting and enjoying the garden and waiting for bus to arrive

more transportation-oriented. She added front-yard seating on Burton Street for people waiting for transportation on the bus.

The California Department of Transportation granted the Historical Society money for the down payment. That grant allowed them to get a loan, buy a cashier's check for my auction price, to prove they had the money, and bid for me on the courthouse steps. When the auction was over, I belonged to the Society!

Be sure to visit the permanent exhibit on the construction of Highway One in my display room.

Enjoy the garden while waiting for a bus to arrive.

Read the tourist information on the kiosk.

These amenities may be the reason I am not now a parking lot!

10

Reconstruction

After I my sale to the Cambria Historical Society at the auction in 2001, I had care and respect.

Fundraising events paid for my repair. Cambrians bought cuttings of roses and other plants from my garden. Fence pickets with brass name plaques and walkway bricks inscribed with the names of family members were sold. Members kept up a stream of donations. The Hind Foundation, an organization that funds projects to restore historical buildings, made a generous grant.

I celebrated! I was not to be torn down. All kinds of people came to study me. Archeologists dug in my cellar and water well and cataloged artifacts. Architects studied and documented my structure to figure out which rooms were built first. Volunteers scraped my walls to reveal original wallpaper to be copied. People took samples of my boards and trim details to be taken to a mill for replication. Volunteers moved plants to safe places.

Here at age 131 years, people fussed over me!

A plan to restore me was in place. Not much of the original Clendenen's one room "salt box" was repairable. The termites and dry rot had taken their toll. They took me apart with care and numbered and cataloged the pieces. To my great surprise, they jacked me up eight feet above ground, off my rock foundation. I didn't like that. At my age, it is not nice to be perched high on wooden blocks.

House jacked up eight feet to build foundation

Archeologists dug around under me for artifacts. Then, a new modern reinforced concrete foundation was poured for me to sit upon. When they sat me back down on the new foundation, it felt good: firm and even. I was back!

Because I would now be a museum, with crowds walking through me, they strengthen my floors and to meet current building codes. The flooring in my fireplace room had rotted away by the rain that had poured through my leaky roof.

I am now wheelchair assessable. Eugenio Bianchini would have liked that.

My parlor around 1890 when the Gutheries lived in me

About 1890, when Sarah lived in me, someone took a photograph of my parlor. The Cambria Historical Society has restored my parlor to look like that picture, duplicating the style of furniture, curtains, light fixtures, wallpaper, and picture rail. They filled me with antique furniture representing that era. Sarah Gutherie would like that.

A picture of me today, the Cambria Historical Museum. In 2008, my restoration was completed, I opened to the public. Here I am, 137 years old, painted, and more beautiful than ever.

Now, l I have a very extensive family. They fought to keep me from being demolished and then raised money to buy me. Scores of people volunteered to preserve details of construction. They preserved and restored my garden.

A picture of me today as the Cambria Historical Museum

If you visit me, Docents tell my history.

Consider that you are not only visiting a house. You are visiting the past and present community of Cambria.

So, this is my story, an American story. I had humble beginnings, and now I am a respected and contributing part of my community.

The People Who Owned Me

Thomas C. Clendenen   1869–1870

Bought lots and constructed me as a one-room house.

E. Apsey & Winfield S. Whitaker   1871–1873

Local businessmen who bought me as a real estate speculation and added a lean-to room on the north side of me for a bedroom (Later removed during remodels) and the porch on the Center Street side. The shape of the house referred to as "salt box" after the similar New England style.

Leonidas B. Root   1873–1882

Mr. and Mrs. Root lived in me for 9 years.

Benjamin H. Franklin   1882–1883

Attorney, businessman, and real estate speculator who added my parlor, two bedrooms (now used as the gift shop and exhibit room) the front and back porch and the fireplace, window, and interior trim.   (The Historical Society restored me to the basic shape I was in 1883).

Sarah Woods Guthrie   1883–1916

Planted my gardens, furnished and decorated me.

Eugenio and Louisa Bizzini Bianchini   1916–1942

Enclosed my east (back) porch and made it into food preparation kitchen. Eugenio died two years after his wife and his estate was held in a trust.

Estate in probates   1942–1999

House occupied by Bianchini children, including "Weasel," who died in 1952, "Coyote" who died in 1959, and "Spider," who died in 1971. I was used for storage and then abandoned. After 1971, my ownership was tied up in a sequence of probates and resulting litigation.

Cambria Historical Society buys me   2001

Opened in my restored form as the Cambria Historical Museum in 2008.

Acknowledgments

I thank the many people who prevented me from being destroyed and helped bring me back to my restored state. I thank the many historians who kept my story alive, particularly Dawn Dunlap, Bev and Jerry Praver, and the other authors who contributed to the website Cambria History Exchange. Mike Rice has helped to have people understand how my structure changed over time.

I thank the members and officers of the Cambria Historical Society for giving me a new existence as an important member of the community. I am grateful that they could provide the photos used to tell my story. I am indebted to the many volunteers who maintain me and my beloved gardens. I appreciate the docents who give visitors my history.

I thank Dawn Dunlap, Gayle Oksen, Marge Sewell, Rick Hawley, and Bev and Jerry Praver for their careful review of my story and for filling in the parts of my story I didn't remember well.

Dedication

To Dawn Dunlap.
Keeping Cambria history alive

About Ken Renshaw

I live with the love of my life, Joyce, at the edge of a pine forest, overlooking the ocean, watching whales, and listening to the sound of the surf, in Cambria, California.

I am the third generation of Renshaw's to Live in Cambria.

We are both active in the community affairs of this small town. We are life members of the Cambria Historical Society where Joyce is a docent.

I am grateful to of the Cambria Rough Writers Group who helped me polish this manuscript, and to David Strom who made a helpful review.

I have published a number of other books. (See kenrenshaw.com)

www.ingramcontent.com/pod-product-compliance
Lightning Source LLC
Chambersburg PA
CBHW060955120626
46557CB00003B/1165